SECRETS OF THE STONE

HARRIET PECK TAYLOR

FARRAR STRAUS GIROUX   NEW YORK

Distributed in Canada by Douglas & McIntyre Ltd.

Color separations by Prestige Graphics

Printed and bound in the United States of America by Phoenix Color Corp.

Typography by Rebecca A. Smith

First edition, 2000

1 3 5 7 9 10 8 6 4 2

Library of Congress Cataloging-in-Publication Data

Taylor, Harriet Peck.

Secrets of the stone / Harriet Peck Taylor. — 1st ed.

p. cm.

Summary: While chasing Jackrabbit, Coyote and Badger come upon a cave filled
with wondrous drawings.

ISBN 0-374-36648-9

[1. Cave paintings—Fiction.   2. Pueblo Indians—Fiction.   3. Indians of North
America—Southwest, New—Fiction.   4. Animals—Fiction.]   I. Title.

PZ7.T2135Se   2000

[E]—dc21   99-41363

To Cathy,

for your strength, courage, and caring

In the old days, when hunting was poor, Coyote and Badger sometimes hunted together. Badger was a strong-pawed, long-clawed, handsome fellow, while Coyote was clever and bold and could run faster than tumbleweed in a windstorm. Their home was the desert. Mesas and buttes rose up off the land like silent stone giants. Rivers and creeks twisted through narrow canyons.

Late one afternoon, Coyote and Badger were hunting along a small creek surrounded by sandstone cliffs. Off in the distance, they saw Jackrabbit hopping merrily along.

"Over there," whispered Coyote as he dashed forward.

Jackrabbit bounded easily out of reach. "So you think you'll have me for dinner, do you? We'll see about that!" he exclaimed.

Coyote and Badger finally cornered Jackrabbit, but just when they thought they had him, he slipped through an opening between a boulder and the cliff wall. Inside, they could hear Jackrabbit laughing. "Hah! Hah! Hah! Hah!"

"Badger, dig under the boulder to loosen it while I lean on it," said Coyote.

Plunk! Thunk! Whunk! With his strong paws, Badger sent the dirt flying. Coyote heaved and pushed with all his might. Then the boulder rolled, and they found themselves at the entrance to a hidden cave.

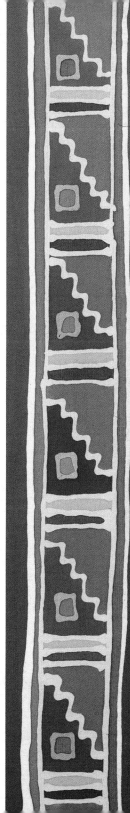

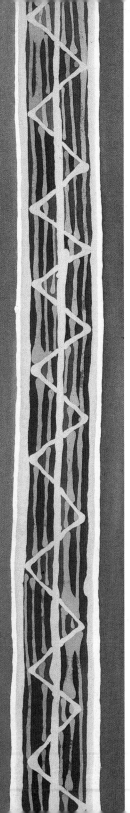

They stared in amazement as the sun's last rays revealed paintings on the rock walls. There were animals, birds, fish, human figures, and mysterious shapes and signs. Badger and Coyote forgot all about the chase.

Coyote was so excited that he began to yip and bark and finally sent a long howl rolling down the canyon. "*Oooowwwaaaah.*"

Soon Antelope appeared in a cloud of dust. "What's all the fuss about?" she asked. Then she saw the rock art and moved forward to touch it with her slender hoof.

Up on the canyon rim, Bighorn Sheep was sleeping. Coyote's howl woke him, and he decided to investigate. When he poked his head inside the cave, his eyes grew big and wide.

"Come in, my friend," said Badger. "Don't you think that picture looks like your grandfather?" He chuckled, pointing at one of the pictures of an animal with curled horns.

"And that looks like Antelope's cousin, Deer," said Coyote. "There's our good friend Mountain Lion." Coyote grinned. "You can tell by his long tail. And this one has got to be a distant relative of Jackrabbit's. He's got the same big feet!"

"These look like the tracks of our great Bear," added Antelope.

"How mysterious they are," whispered Bighorn. "I wonder who made them and what they mean."

"Perhaps they were made by our ancestors as they traveled through this area," answered Badger. "They may have wanted to show others that they had been here."

"Could the artists have been trying to speak to the spirit world?" asked Antelope.

"I feel as if they're talking to us," said Badger.

"You're imagining things," said Coyote.

Suddenly the clouds turned black and the wind came up in gusts that sent the cottonwood leaves twirling madly through the twilight sky.

"I think we're in for a storm," said Bighorn. "Let's wait it out in the cave."

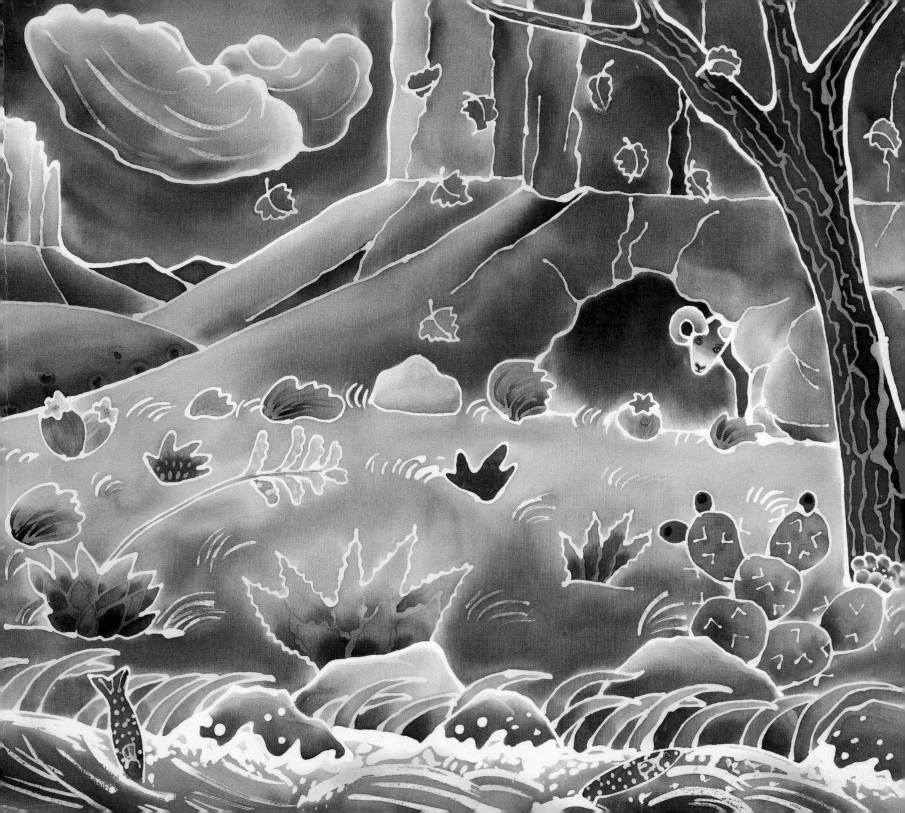

They got a warm fire going and huddled around it. In the flickering firelight, the pictures appeared to move and almost jump off the cave wall. Ghostly figures with clawlike hands and masked faces seemed to sway and dance.

Then they heard a muffled sound behind the stone wall. *Scratch. Scratch.*

"I'm afraid," whispered Antelope.

"Maybe our ancestors *are* trying to reach us," said Badger.

"Oh, that was only a tree branch brushing against the side of the canyon wall," said Bighorn.

Next they heard a high-pitched whistle.

"There are powerful spirits in this cave," whined Antelope.

"Hmm," said Badger. "I don't think that's what spirits sound like."

"Don't worry. I'm here to protect us," said Coyote.

Antelope still looked worried and drew closer to the fire. Bighorn sang a little song to help calm their nerves. Over and over he sang the song, until the fire burned to glowing embers.

At last they settled down to sleep. Coyote tucked his face into his big, bushy tail and soon was dreaming.

Coyote found himself racing through a star-filled night. Bighorn sheep drifted by on a distant mesa, their horns curled against the sky.

A small herd of deer wandered past.

Traveling deeper into the night, Coyote saw a mountain lion glide by swiftly and silently on big cat paws.

Coyote watched as two antelope disappeared over the canyon rim.

On a rocky ridge, hunters carried brightly painted shields. They followed the antelope.

Much closer, but just out of reach, a bear left huge tracks in the wet sand on the riverbank. In the river, a heron stood on long, skinny legs. Silvery fish flipped and flopped in the moonlit water.

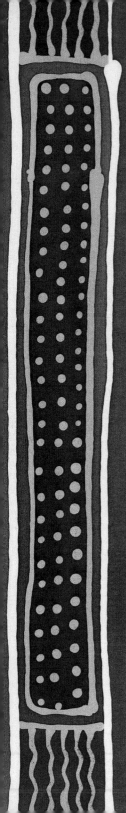

A ghostly spirit floated toward Coyote above the desert sands. He had horns and held a snake over his head. As the spirit looked his way, Coyote trembled, then hurried on through the night.

Coyote was drawn to dancers wearing strange masks and robes. Chanting and singing, they twisted and turned in a line like a giant rattlesnake.

Beyond, high on a hill, a flute player danced. His song was carried on the wind. Its beauty drew Coyote near. Caught up in the magic of the melody, Coyote found himself dancing.

Then, down in the valley, he saw a jackrabbit. The jackrabbit bounded up the hill and down the hill, along the ridge and across a creek. Coyote ran and ran in pursuit, but never seemed to get any closer.

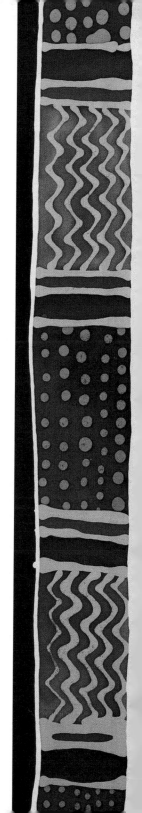

Coyote found himself back in the cool, dark cave. The paintings were still and silent, and Badger was shaking him. Bighorn and Antelope were looking at him with puzzled faces.

"Wake up, Coyote," said Badger. "Your paws were twitching, and you were yipping in your sleep."

"I was running all night in a faraway land," said Coyote. "The pictures came off the rock wall and were real. I saw animals, birds, fish, hunters, dancers, and a mysterious flute player. Then I was chasing a jackrabbit, but couldn't catch him."

Before anyone could say another word, they heard a familiar scratch, followed by a high-pitched whistle and the unmistakable sound of laughter.

"Jackrabbit!" said Badger.

At that moment, Jackrabbit bounded toward the cave entrance.

"Come on!" said Coyote, and the two hunters resumed the chase.

Many years have come and gone since then, but every so often, when the moon first appears above some distant butte, Coyote hears the flute player's haunting melody, a song from long ago and far away. At those times, he feels sure that the Ancient Ones reached out across the years to show him the secrets of the stone.

AUTHOR'S NOTE

Scattered throughout the Southwestern United States, as well as in many other places in the world, early humans left a record of their life in the form of pictures on rocks. There are two different kinds of rock art: petroglyphs and pictographs. Petroglyphs were carved into the rock; pictographs were painted onto the rock.

The earliest rock art of the Southwest was made by nomadic tribes which traveled in small bands, hunting game and gathering wild food. At some point, they began to farm and settled down in the high desert region.

The setting of this story is the northern part of the American Southwest. Most of the rock art represented is that of the early inhabitants of the area, the Ancestral Puebloans, formerly known as the Anasazi. Their culture flourished here until around 1300, when problems arose (possibly drought or warfare) that made them move elsewhere.

Many images appear in the rock art: animals, birds, human forms, spirits, the moon, stars, sun, clouds, rain, and more. One of the most fascinating figures is the humpbacked flute player. Known as Kokopelli, he is thought of variously as a trickster, a magician, a wandering minstrel, or a rain priest.

What do the rock pictures mean? They may have been created to give power to a hunt or to cause crops to grow, to protect against evil forces or to show migration of people from one place to another. We will never know exactly. Still, these pictures draw us in as if by magic and speak powerfully of a time and place we can only imagine.

SOURCES

America's Fascinating Indian Heritage. Pleasantville, N.Y.: The Reader's Digest Association, Inc., 1978.

Cunkle, James R., and Markus A. Jacquemain. *Stone Magic of the Ancients: Petroglyphs, Shamanic Shrine Sites, Ancient Rituals*. Phoenix, Ariz.: Golden West Publishers, 1995.

Patterson, Alex. *A Field Guide to Rock Art Symbols of the Greater Southwest*. Boulder, Colo.: Johnson Books, 1992.

Slifer, Dennis, and James Duffield. *Kokopelli: Fluteplayer Images in Rock Art*. Santa Fe, N.Mex.: Ancient City Press, 1994.

Thybony, Scott. *Rock Art of the American Southwest*. Portland, Oreg.: Graphic Arts Center Publishing, 1994.